Goodbye, Ms. Parker

{ NICE TO READ YOU! }

Goodbye, Ms. Parker

Telma Guimarães

Ilustrações de Weberson Santiago

Editora do Brasil

© Editora do Brasil S.A., 2014
Todos os direitos reservados
Texto © Telma Guimarães
Ilustrações © Weberson Santiago

DIREÇÃO EXECUTIVA Maria Lúcia Kerr Cavalcante Queiroz
DIREÇÃO EDITORIAL Cibele Mendes Curto Santos
GERÊNCIA EDITORIAL Felipe Ramos Poletti
SUPERVISÃO DE ARTE E EDITORAÇÃO Adelaide Carolina Cerutti
SUPERVISÃO DE CONTROLE DE PROCESSOS EDITORIAIS Marta Dias Portero
SUPERVISÃO DE DIREITOS AUTORAIS Marilisa Bertolone Mendes
SUPERVISÃO DE REVISÃO Dora Helena Feres
EDIÇÃO Gilsandro Vieira Sales
ASSISTÊNCIA EDITORIAL Flora Vaz Manzione
AUXÍLIO EDITORIAL Paulo Fuzinelli
COORDENAÇÃO DE ARTE Maria Aparecida Alves
PRODUÇÃO DE ARTE Obá Editorial
    COORDENAÇÃO Simone Oliveira
    EDIÇÃO Mayara Menezes do Moinho
    PROJETO GRÁFICO E DIAGRAMAÇÃO Thaís Gaal Rupeika
COORDENAÇÃO DE REVISÃO Otacilio Palareti
REVISÃO Equipe EBSA
CONTROLE DE PROCESSOS EDITORIAIS Leila P. Jungstedt e Bruna Alves

DADOS INTERNACIONAIS DE CATALOGAÇÃO NA PUBLICAÇÃO (CIP)
(CÂMARA BRASILEIRA DO LIVRO, SP, BRASIL)

Andrade, Telma Guimarães Castro
   Goodbye, Ms, Parker/Telma Guimarães; ilustrações de Weberson Santiago. – 2. ed. – São Paulo: Editora do Brasil, 2014. – (Nice to read you!)

   ISBN 978-85-10-05472-0

   1. Inglês (Ensino fundamental) I. Santiago, Weberson. II. Título. III. Série.

14-06929   CDD-372.652

ÍNDICES PARA CATÁLOGO SISTEMÁTICO:
1. Inglês : Ensino fundamental   372.652

2ª edição / 1ª impressão, 2014
Impresso na Intergraf Ind. Gráfica Eirelli

Rua Conselheiro Nébias, 887
São Paulo, SP, CEP 01203-001
Fone (11) 3226-0211 – Fax (11) 3222-5583
www.editoradobrasil.com.br

Mr. Simpson entered the bedroom.

He took off his coat and looked at Ms. Parker's body.

There were still pieces of wood burning in the fireplace.

He took his pipe from the left pocket and lit it.

"At my age, a man needs to be retired… Don't you agree, Ms. Hill?", he asked the maid who was standing beside the door.

"Oh, you're still… young!" Ms. Hill tried to be polite.

"She *was* very vain, wasn't she?" He stared at the bottles of perfume, silver hair brushes, wrinkle cream on the lady's dressing table. "And diabetic, perhaps?" he asked.

"Yes, Mr. Simpson," the maid agreed.

"A very vain woman with many jewels…" He walked in circles, smoking his pipe. "She hasn't combed her hair, Ms. Hill, has she?" He looked at the dead woman's hair.

"Well, she certainly didn't know she would have a crisis, Mr. Simpson."

"Yes, you're right. She couldn't realize she would die the way she did."

"I beg your pardon, Mr.…," said the young lady.

The door bell rang once more.

Ms. Hill left the room.

She had to go downstairs to open the door.

"I don't know why she had to die today. It's Saturday! It's my free day," she said upset. *"Ms. Hill, I told you to take these letters to the post office, but it seems you're a perfect dumb. What did you put in this soup? You'll never learn, you will always be a maid!"* She tried to imitate the woman's voice.

"I can't lie to myself. I'm glad she has passed away. She wasn't polite. She was so... so... so mean, selfish, rude, and..." Ms. Hill couldn't avoid smiling.

She was almost happy.

Ms. Hill opened the door. It was Dr. Parker, Ms. Parker's nephew.

"I came as soon as I knew." He was very pale.

I really like him. He's my type. Nice looking, tall, many muscles, rich, blue eyes, blond hair… Unluckily, I'm not his kind. Poor and now… UNEMPLOYED, she thought.

"It was her asthma, wasn't it?" Alan Parker asked the maid.

"I don't know… She died like a small sparrow." She hung the man's coat on the hat stand. "Maybe the doctor upstairs can tell you the right time…" She smiled in a sweet manner.

"Oh, there's another doctor upstairs with… the body!" He took a handkerchief to dry the tears.

Poor Dr. Parker… He's suffering because of that insane woman, thought Ms. Hill.

"The body… I mean, Ms. Parker is still on her bed. It seems as if she's still sleeping…"

"Oh, Ms. Hill, she was everything I had. I became a doctor because of her help." Dr. Parker shook his head.

"I can understand, Dr. Parker. I'll miss her too. I loved her, you know," she said. The maid tried to look natural, but her voice sounded false.

"Well, I'll have to talk to the doctor. Thank you, Ms. Hill. You're so sweet." Dr. Parker kissed the maid's hands. "I don't know how I can thank you for all the love you devoted to auntie."

"Ten years, sir. Ten years," she answered.

But the man was gone.

"He didn't hear me! Asthma... Diabetes... I thought she was as strong as a bull... The *old snake*," she kept on saying on her way to the kitchen.

Mr. Simpson looked at the man.

"Good morning... I'm Dr. Alan Parker," the man introduced himself. "Oh, poor auntie." Dr. Alan Parker kneeled down by his aunt's bed. "Aunt Emily! She didn't have enough time to eat her apple…" He looked at the apple that was near her left hand.

"Please, Dr. Parker, nothing here may be touched," Mr. Simpson started to talk. "I'm Detective Simpson."

"*Detective*? I thought you were a doctor! Ms. Hill told me there was a…"

"Oh, I see! Well, *there was* a doctor here… Dr. Draper… But he has already gone," he started to explain. "Shall we go downstairs?"

Alan Parker was very surprised. As soon as they entered Ms. Parker's office, he fell down on the armchair.

"I can't understand! What really happened? She was so fine yesterday afternoon! I came here to have lunch with her… We walked through the park… She even told me a joke!" He could hardly breathe.

"It seems she had asthma." Mr. Simpson opened a drawer and took a small book.

"So, what are you…"

"Doing here? Well, Dr. Parker, where there's smoke…" He let out a big cloud of smoke from his pipe.

"You mean *somebody*… Oh, not her! She was kind and…" — Dr. Parker suddenly stood up when he heard somebody shouting.

"Ms. Parker, Ms. Parker! I'll call the police this time! I'll kill you!" the man kept on shouting.

"See? She wasn't *that* kind," smiled Mr. Simpson.

"Shhh!" Ms. Hill tried to calm down the man. "She's gone, don't you understand?"

"She's gone with my violets. She cut them off! Can you believe that?" The poor neighbor was almost crying. "I can bet it was the day before yesterday… Maybe yesterday afternoon. I thought I could see her flower hat behind the lilies… *I'll kill that snake!*"

"Hum, hum," Mr. Simpson murmured, opening the office door.

Ms. Hill was very pale. She didn't know they were downstairs.

"Who is this man?" Mr. Fields wanted to know. "Maybe *the snake*... I mean, Ms. Parker cut his flowers, too!" he whispered to Ms. Hill.

The lady was very embarrassed. She tried to explain to the old man that the woman had passed away, but it seemed he was deaf.

"I'm Mr. Simpson, sir," the detective introduced himself.

"My aunt hasn't done any damage to your flowers, Mr. Fields." Dr. Parker spoke in a low-pitched voice. "*She died,*" the lady's nephew explained.

"What?" Mr. Fields was staggered.

Detective Simpson gently pushed the old man to the office and led him to an armchair.

"Would you sit down, please?" he asked.

"I'll bring you a cup of tea, Mr. Simpson."

Ms. Hill could hardly disguise a smile of satisfaction.

"The diabetes, I suppose?" He was very pale and uneasy.

Ms. Hill tried to stay in the office in order to listen to the conversation, but Mr. Simpson stared at her so deeply that she decided to go make the tea she had promised the man.

As soon as she left the office, Detective Simpson continued the explanation:

"Well, she probably died of diabetes... Or asthma... Or probably not." He lit his pipe again.

"What do you mean with *probably not*? Could it be an ulcer?" Mr. Fields was still pale.

Detective Simpson smiled.

"Dr. Parker, would you mind...?" he didn't finish the question.

Dr. Parker understood and left the office to phone the priest. He was trying to be practical, but his heart was small. He felt as if life had tied his heart in knots... Emily was all he had... And now she was gone.

He hung up the phone and left the house. He would walk in the garden and talk to himself. He would feel better, he knew that. He was going to wait for the priest, his aunt's best friend.

Detective Simpson and Mr. Fields started a conversation then.

"Well, you may count on me, Mr. Fields. There's no problem if you did not get along well with her. See, I don't like one of my neighbors. He has twelve cats. I just hate cats!" He sat down in the sofa.

"You really think she was *mur...* *murdered*?" Mr. Fields coughed. "But why?

See, I was joking when I said I'd kill her!" The old man was nervous.

"I can understand." Detective Simpson stood up to look through the window.

Near the front gate there were two or three people — maybe neighbors —, pointing at the house. Ms. Hill talking to them.

A talkative maid. And she didn't like Ms. Parker either, Detective Simpson thought to himself.

"Well, Mr. Fields, I must do my job..." Detective Simpson started to talk.

"You mean, you are going to ask me a few questions, sir?" The man was very anxious.

"Yes, if you don't mind." Detective Simpson took a small notebook from his pocket. "How many years ago did you break up with Ms. Parker?" he asked suddenly.

The old man tried to open his mouth to say something, but he couldn't.

How did the detective know? Nobody knew they had been engaged *more than forty years ago! Only his wife, but it was a long time since she had passed away*, he thought.

"Mr. Fields, you don't have to hide anything from me. I'm not going to arrest you!" Detective Simpson laughed at the poor man.

Not now, at least! Mr. Fields thought to himself.

"How did you find that out? Nobody knew!" The man stood up and started walking around the desk.

"Well, it was not hard... The lady had a picture in her medallion." Detective Simpson stopped in front of the back window, pulling the white curtains.

"Had it got my name on the photograph?"

"No... But I could see the spot in your forehead with my lens... And she still kept the ring with three initials... *Edward George Fields... E.G.F. Your initials.* It was in her drawer."

"She had never forgiven me. I left her because of Annie. Annie was sweet, kind...

She was not so demanding. When I heard she had bought the house beside ours, I knew it was on purpose. She had pleasure in disturbing our peace, our home... *And I hated her for that.* Why couldn't she just forget the past? So many years have passed by... Why has her hatred lasted so long? I haven't killed her, detective. I would have killed her before... but I couldn't. She was right. I am a weak man." Mr. Fields took off his glasses.

Someone knocked at the door.

"Come in", said Mr. Simpson.

Ms. Hill entered with two cups of tea. She also brought some French rolls.

"Do you feel better, Mr. Fields?" She winked at him.

"Yes, Ms. Hill. I'm fine," he answered

"Oh, thank you very much, Ms. Hill. You're so *efficient*, aren't you?"

Detective Simpson praised her. "Mr. Fields, while we drink this nice tea, would you please go to my car in the garage and pick up my monocle? I can't write well without changing my glasses..." he asked the man.

Ms. Hill was very pale.

As soon as Mr. Fields left the office, Ms. Hill tried to leave the place, but she couldn't.

"Nice bracelet, Ms. Hill..." Detective Simpson remarked.

"Thanks, sir. It was my mother's..." The maid started to explain.

"Ms. Parker wouldn't have approved of that..." Detective Simpson touched the bracelet with his walking stick.

The maid felt very uncomfortable.

"I don't understand, sir!" She looked right into his eyes.

"Oh, you do... *You stole this bracelet*. It was Ms. Parker's. There's a ring like this in the safe, Ms. Hill..." He smiled.

"Oh, I didn't know..." She twisted the gold jewelry around her wrist. "But she would have given it to me... She liked me... She told me once. Are you going to arrest me, sir? I didn't kill her!" She took the bracelet off and put it on the desk. "Here's the jewelry... You're right. I stole it... Well, that snake wouldn't give me anything at all... *Ms. Hill... Are you dumb?*" Ms. Hill made a funny voice and fell down on the armchair.

Mr. Simpson kept on writing in his notebook.

"Do you know this book?" He showed Ms. Hill a small green book.

"Of course I do. It's Ms. Parker's favorite book of proverbs." She tidied up her apron.

"I bet she liked it", Detective Simpson opened it.

"By the way, Ms. Hill, was Ms. Parker used to taking her insulin three times a day?"

"Oh, no, Mr. Simpson. I already told the doctor this morning! She was used to taking it twice a day... She could never take insulin three times a day, otherwise she'd die. Ask the doctor, please. He will tell you."

"Were you used to giving her the medicine?" He pointed his walking stick at her.

"Yes, but yesterday... She told me to go to the post office after lunch. She wanted me to mail an envelope. Do you mean... I'm under suspicion?" She bit her lips.

"Well, what would you think if you were in my place?" He shook his walking stick.

"I don't know. I told her, detective, she ate too much during lunch."

"Have you made her something special?" He wanted to know.

"Steak, mashed potatoes, salad… And cheese cake. They didn't leave a piece."

"They?"

"She and her nephew. He had lunch with her."

"Oh, I see."

Someone knocked at the door.

"Come in," said Detective Simpson.

"I couldn't find your monocle, detective," stammered Mr. Fields.

"Well, it doesn't matter, Mr. Fields. I'm almost… finished." He smiled at Ms. Hill. "Come in, Mr. Fields and drink your tea. Maybe you can try some of these French rolls", he offered.

"I don't think I'm hungry," the man refused the offer.

"Me neither," said Dr. Parker, approaching the open door. "May I come in?" he asked.

"Sure," replied Detective Simpson.

"What are they going to do now?" Ms. Hill wanted to know.

"You must tell the priest that the service will have to wait," the detective interrupted the sentence. "We are going to have an autopsy."

"I can't understand!" Dr. Parker couldn't believe that. "She probably died of an asthma attack!"

"He doesn't think so!" Ms. Hill stood up. "He thinks *I gave her* more insulin than usual!" She left the room very nervous.

Dr. Parker was worried.

"Do you really think she could do that?" he asked the detective.

"Maybe. She was here after dinner, wasn't she?"

"I don't know. When I left she was watering the plants. I saw her. I said good-bye to her. She even answered. Maybe you're right!" he exclaimed. "Ms. Hill calls her a 'snake'".

"Well, let us see the doctor's final report. Poison, who knows?" he said with a smile.

Nobody answered. Not even Ms. Hill, who was very still behind the door, listening to that conversation.

The service was nice. There came Mr. Ford, the priest, some neighbors, the mailman, the milkman, the owner of the grocery, Ms. Parker's lawyer and, of course, Dr. Parker and Ms. Hill. Mr. Fields didn't show up.

Now, the lady could finally rest in peace.

The doctor had already given the report to Detective Simpson.

"Nothing. 'Cause of death': diabetes. That was all."

But he wouldn't give up! He started reading his notes again.

An apple. That didn't fit.

He remembered the proverb: An apple a day keeps the doctor… away! That was it!

It was so clear!

Mr. Simpson decided to wait. He knew who had killed the poor lady. Although she was not poor. She was a very rude--mannered woman. A very bitter and unforgiving one. She had lost her only true love. Her parents had died when she was very young. In spite of all that, she had been very rich. Detective Simpson had taken a look at her will.

"… and I leave everything I have to my only nephew, the stepson of my dearest younger sister Rachel, Alan Parker, MD."

"Well, she tried to change that. And she could have. She was smart." He'd have loved her. Maybe he'd have married that woman… Ms. Parker. He liked smart women. Unfortunately she was gone. "That was a pity!" he regretted.

Two days after the funeral, Mr. Simpson called up the three suspects. The case was over.

"The apple," he started, "there was an apple beside the body… It wasn't her favorite proverb: 'An apple a day keeps the doctor away'. It happens that she didn't like apples. Why then, would she have pulled the tray with fruit and taken just the apple? She'd rather take a peach or a pear… Why? Because she knew right at that moment he was killing her. She was having an insulin overdose. He'd have to give her a certain amount of insulin and what did he do? He gave her much more than she'd have taken herself. In fifteen, maybe sixteen minutes, she would be dead. She'd have called Ms. Hill, but she was feeling weaker and weaker… Besides, she had sent Ms. Hill to the post office! While her nephew — *you, Dr. Alan Parker,* — kept on talking slowly, telling her sweet things, maybe things about your childhood... Am I wrong?"

After a moment, Detective Simpson went on speaking:

"I bet I'm not! She probably understood that it was too late. But not that much... As soon as he left, and he thought she was already dead, she caught the apple and bit it... *An apple a day keeps the doctor away...* That's what I figured out! He knew she could change the testament... She'd know he was out of money. He was broke. He owed a lot of money and he'd be in jail if she didn't help him. It so happened that he'd never let her know. She hated gambling. She'd never lend him any money. So, when *you, Dr. Alan Parker,* when you figured out she needed her daily

insulin, you decided to overload her... And she knew that. But it was too late! Almost! Poor woman! She ate too much... And you were the one responsible! You could have stopped her... You knew she was eating too much and that she'd have a crisis after so much food! You did nothing but eat with her and wait for her request... *Dear Alan, would you please...,* — your aunt asked you."

"No!" cried Alan Parker.

"*Would you please take my insulin and...*"

"Oh, you can't prove it! You can't!" Alan Parker was totally pale.

"Yes, I can." Detective Simpson opened his suitcase.

Dr. Parker didn't wait for the evidence. He tried to escape, but three policemen were already waiting for him outside. He had no chance.

Ms. Hill was happy. She was sorry for Dr. Parker. Maybe she'd visit him in jail someday, during her day off.

She was wondering where she would find a good job. Ms. Parker hadn't left her even a silver ring…

"Oh, you're a lucky lady, Ms. Hill!" Detective Simpson said, pointing his walking stick at her.

"What do you mean, sir?" She opened her eyes wide.

"The testament says that *'in case of a non-natural death, this cannot be considered a valid testament. The valid one will be laid with Mr…'* Oh, where are my glasses?" Detective Simpson couldn't read the lawyer's letter. "In that testament, the house is totally yours, including everything in it and…" Poor Ms. Hill! She couldn't stand that and fainted.

"Well, what's she going to do when I tell her the garden will be left to you, Mr. Fields?" he asked the neighbor.

"Oh, that... *lovely snake!*" The old man could finally breathe. "By the way, what's the evidence you had against Dr. Parker?" Mr. Fields was very curious.

"That was a joke! When I have none, I tell that! It can work... And it did!"

"I can't believe that!"

"Neither can I!" Detective Simpson laughed and looked at Dr. Parker, who was leaving the house in a police car.

Yes, I'd have loved her, he thought while he looked at her oil painting beside the books in her office.

In the lady's young eyes, he could feel a brightness of youth, a light of a brilliant woman.

Glossary }

In alphabetical order

		dressing table	penteadeira
although	embora	**dumb**	estúpido(a); burro(a)
amount	quantidade		
armchair	poltrona	**fireplace**	lareira
as if	como se	**forehead**	testa
asthma	asma	**French roll**	pãozinho francês doce
at least	pelo menos		
besides	além disso; além do mais	**front gate**	portão da frente
		gambling	jogo de azar
bracelet	pulseira	**grocery**	mercearia
brightness	briho	**handkerchief**	lenço
by the way	a propósito		
childhood	infância		
damage	dano; estrago		
day off	dia livre; dia de folga		
deaf	surdo(a)		
dearest	mais querido(a)		
demanding	exigente		
drawer	gaveta		

		rude-mannered woman	mulher de maneiras rudes
hat stand	cabideiro	safe	cofre
hatred	ódio	selfish	egoísta
in order to	a fim de	service	serviço fúnebre; cerimônia religiosa
in spite of	apesar de		
jail	cadeia	She would rather (She'd rather)	ela preferiria
lawyer	advogado		
lilies	lírios	sparrow	pardal
low-pitched	em tom baixo	spot	mancha; marca
maid	empregada	stepson	filho adotivo; enteado
mashed potatoes	purê de batatas		
mean	malvado(a); miserável	still	quieto(a)
		talkative	tagarela
oil painting	quadro a óleo	to arrest	prender
on purpose	de propósito	to avoid	evitar
otherwise	caso contrário; senão		
pale	pálido		
pipe	cachimbo		
poison	veneno		
priest	padre; sacerdote		
report	relatório		
right into	diretamente		

to be engaged	estar noivo(a); comprometido(a)
to bet	apostar
to bite	morder
to break up	terminar; romper
to call up	telefonar
to comb	pentear
to cough	tossir
to count on	contar com
to disguise	disfarçar
to faint	desmaiar
to figure out	imaginar; perceber
to find out	descobrir
to fit	encaixar
to forgive	perdoar
to get along (with)	dar-se bem (com)
to give up	desistir
to hung up	desligar (telefone)
to kneel down	ajoelhar-se
to lay	colocar; pôr
to lead	conduzir
to lend	emprestar

to lie	mentir
to matter	importar; ter importância
to mean	querer dizer; significar
to mind	importar-se
to murder	assassinar
to overload	sobrecarregar
to owe	dever (dinheiro, favor)
to pass away	morrer
to pick up	apanhar; pegar
to praise	elogiar
to pull	puxar

		to tie one's heart in knots	sentir-se ansioso; com o coração apertado
		to twist	girar
		to whisper	sussurrar
		to wink (at)	piscar
		to wonder	querer saber; imaginar
		to work	dar certo; funcionar
		under suspicion	sob suspeita
to push	empurrar	uneasy	ansioso
to realize	imaginar; fazer ideia	unemployed	desempregado(a)
		unforgiving	rancoroso(a)
to retire	aposentar-se	upset	preocupada; aflita
to show up	aparecer; comparecer	vain	vaidosa
		walking stick	bengala
to stagger	deixar confuso(a); surpreender	weak	fraco
		will	testamento
to stammer	gaguejar	wrinkle	ruga
to stand	aguentar; suportar	wrist	pulso
to steal	roubar	youth	juventude
to take off	tirar		
to tidy up	pôr em ordem		

About the author...

Telma Guimarães is a Brazilian writer of books for children and young people. She graduated in Portuguese and English, which explains why she loves writing in these languages. She loves literature and books, and she has already published a lot of good, fun, and creative stories. Telma lives in Campinas, a city in the state of São Paulo, Brazil. She is married and a mother of three kids. She also has a granddaughter, with whom she shares a lot of stories.

About the illustrator...

Weberson Santiago was born in São Bernardo do Campo, in 1983. He was raised in Mauá and lived for some time in São Paulo, but nowadays he lives in Mogi das Cruzes. Besides illustrating books, Weberson also writes. He teaches at the University of Mogi das Cruzes and at Quanta Academia de Artes.

Este livro foi composto com a família tipográfica
Stone Informal Std, para a Editora do Brasil, em junho de 2014.

Goodbye, Ms. Parker

Telma Guimarães

Suplemento de Atividades

Elaborado por Rodrigo Mendonça

NOME: _____
ANO: _____
ESCOLA: _____

Ms. Parker is dead! She had asthma and diabetes... It was a tragic event. But Detective Simpson thinks that maybe there is something more behind all this. Is Ms. Hill involved in her death? Or, maybe, has Mr. Fields decided to finally get rid of that weed? Or has the apple that she ate been poisoned?

1. Find the answers to the items in the word hunt below.

F	N	U	D	U	M	B	L	U	S	R	O
L	I	L	A	N	D	P	Q	C	T	Z	E
D	E	W	H	I	S	P	E	R	E	O	Y
L	H	E	Z	W	G	D	W	T	L	X	H
A	S	F	V	K	Y	S	M	P	E	A	S
S	F	U	D	I	Q	E	Y	I	C	R	I
T	L	N	L	A	T	I	P	P	A	M	F
H	D	X	S	C	I	A	N	E	R	N	L
M	U	L	L	O	E	B	K	G	B	F	E
A	M	R	X	L	Q	R	E	L	J	K	S
I	D	E	P	Y	E	U	T	P	A	S	B
D	I	A	B	E	T	E	S	A	X	T	U

- A lung problem people should be careful not to lose their breath.
- A jewel people wear in the wrists.
- When people have this disease they should not ingest sugar.
- An offensive term to say somebody is not intelligent.
- People put tobacco inside to smoke, famous detectives love it.
- A person who only thinks of him/herself.
- A person who talks a lot, or likes to gossip.
- People with this stomach problem should avoid spicy and acidic food.
- Said in a low voice, specially to tell a secret.

2. How well do you remember the characters? Put their initials next to the correct information.

Ms. Parker **(MP)**; Ms. Hill **(MH)**; Detective Simpson **(DS)**;
Dr. Alan Parker **(AP)**; Mr. Fields **(MF)**.

_____ still loved Mr. Fields, which is the reason they fought so much.

_____ is a detective; he loves to smoke his pipe.

_____ inherited the garden, he was surprised and happy.

_____ was engaged to Ms. Parker when they were young.

_____ used to call Ms. Parker "old snake" and imitate her voice.

_____ was a very rich woman, but a lot of people didn't like her.

_____ noticed the apple was a clue to discover the murderer.

_____ inherited the house and everything in it.

_____ was the murderer; he killed Ms. Parker with an overdose of insulin.

3. Ms. Parker had some health problems, like diabetes and asthma. Can you match the following health problems to the recommendations below?

a) I have a cold. ◯ She should not wear blouses or wrap up in a blanket.

b) My sister has a fever. ◯ You should drink lots of liquid and rest a lot.

c) My head hurts. ◯ You should start a diet and try to exercise.

d) I am diabetic. ◯ You should avoid sugar.

e) My brother's asthma is acting up. ◯ You should take an aspirin.

f) I am overweight. ◯ He should quickly call the doctor and try to breathe slowly.

7. Let's learn a little more about character creation? Detective stories need a detective who is intelligent, but in a way we can identify and follow his ideas. Writers can create this effect by giving strong personality traits to their creations. Then choose one of the detectives from exercise 6 and write a paragraph explaining who he is!

For example:

Mr. X is a detective created by book writer Sir Y. He is very cold and calculating, but also very intelligent. He is usually helped by Dr. Z, who helps him during his hypoglycemic crises. Mr. X is secretly in love with Madam A, but they never seem to be honest about their feelings. Mr. X also has a paralyzing fear of clowns, which his archenemy Mr. L uses to torture him.

8. Did you enjoy the end of the story? Did you suspect Doctor Alan Parker? Use the space below and create your own ending! You can change the murderer, the reason, or any other fact you want.

4. And now, create your own recommendations for the problems below using "should".

   a) My mother wants me to change schools, but I don't want to.

   _____
   _____

   b) I want to buy a pet, but my brother is allergic.

   _____
   _____

   c) I broke my mother's vase and I think she will be angry.

   _____
   _____

   d) I am in love with a boy/girl from school, but I think he/she likes my best friend.

   _____
   _____

5. Let's practice giving and receiving advices?

   a) First, create a problem and write it in a separate sheet of paper. It can be a real problem or a problem you have just invented.

   For example:

   I am having a lot of difficulties with the math exercises and nobody can help me

   Now change the sheets with a friend, you will need to create two different recommendations for the problem.

   For example:

   You should ask your parents to help you with the homework.

   Then you should talk to your teacher and be honest; he/she can give you some help.

b) Now you will present the problems for the class. Be prepared because you need to create an objection for the first recommendation. The script below will help you.

For example:

Student 1: – I am having a lot of difficulties with the math exercises and nobody can help me.

Student 2: – You should ask your parents to help you with the homework.

Student 1: Sorry but I cannot do that. (IMPROVISING) Ahn, well… They work a lot!

Student 2: – Then you should talk to your teacher and be honest; he/she can give you some help.

Student 1: That is a great idea, I will do that!

6. There are many famous fictional detectives in literature and on TV. Do you know any of them? Try to match the detectives below to their creators and the stories they appear on.

a) Adrian Monk ⬡ Created by Edgar Allan Poe for "The Murders in the Rue Morgue".

b) Philip Marlowe ⬡ Created by Raymond Chandler in "The Big Sleep".

c) Sherlock Holmes ⬡ Created by Sir Arthur Conan Doyle, first appeared in "A Study in Scarlet".

d) Hercule Poirot ⬡ Created by Andy Breckman for *Monk* (TV series).

e) C. Auguste Dupin ⬡ Created by Agatha Christie in "The Mysterious Affair at Styles".

Do you know any other famous detectives that are not on the list? Who are they? Who created them and on what stories have they appeared?

_____

_____

_____